The Ladder,
The Dream,
and
The Climb

Tambeara Watkins

Watkins Christian Publishing

Also by Tambeara Watkins

Secret Insanity

He Came Home

The Goodbye Series

Take My Running Shoes

The Ladder, The Dream, And The Climb

Adoption Unwind a collection short stories

The Ladder,
The Dream,
and
The Climb

NAMES AND DREAMS

The parents had three daughters and gave proper names to the siblings at the time of their birth, but the names were unsuitable for the siblings because their parents knew the norm would not apply to their children.

After dinner, the parents thanked God for their blessings and asked God for guidance for their children's journey in life.

The parents smiled knowing their prayers had been heard.

That night, God spoke to the parents and told them to build three ladders in their backyard, each three stories high. They were instructed not to share details of the ladders or even acknowledge them. The parents followed the instructions without question, never telling the girls why the ladders were there. They would discover them in their own time.

As the siblings played in the backyard one day, they noticed the ladders. They stopped and stared at them intently, wondering what they were for. Then, as if in answer to their unspoken thoughts, one sibling blurted out, "Let's change our names."

"Yeah," said the first sibling.

"It could be changed to something we love, like our favorite flower."

"Yeah, like a flower name or something," said the next sibling.

"Okay, let's finish playing, and when a name fits us, that will be our new name," said the last sibling.

"Well, I don't know," said the first sibling.

How could we ever choose a name? I mean, I do not want to get it wrong. So, I think I will just wait on God."

"I know I will need someone to help me choose a name," said the next sibling.

"I'm so excited about our new names! Today could be the day," said the last sibling.

They all looked at each other and laughed hard. The siblings had each discovered their new names.

And so, it was set.

From that moment on, the siblings embraced their new names.

THE RIDE

Saturday morning, the siblings couldn't believe their wish of riding a beautiful pink pony would finally come true. At noon, a small trailer pulled up to their front yard, and out stepped a sleek pink pony, its mane braided with ribbons. Help Me, Today Could Be The Day, I'm Just Waiting On God, and their friends squealed and jumped joyfully, imagining themselves riding around the backyard on the back of their perfect pink pony. It was their birthday wish, and the parents had planned the surprise months before.

I'M JUST WAITING ON GOD

From the beginning, as she stood on the side, watching others enjoy the pony, this sibling felt the anticipation. She was in a state of waiting, waiting on God to give her instructions at the perfect moment, believing these things were important. With its beautiful pink coat, the pony trotted around the yard, a symbol of her unfulfilled desire. She longed to climb atop and parade around the yard, but the timing was not in her hands.

So, for now, she could only watch as others had their turn while Help Me tried to encourage her. "Why don't you just get on the pony and ride it?" she yelled.

But I'm Just Waiting On God was determined to wait on God. She knew that God would tell her when the time was right. Hours later, as she marveled at the pony's beauty and then watched it slowly return to its carriage, she felt sad and frustrated. Why did everyone else get their chance to ride while she was left behind? Couldn't God see how much this meant to her?

Her dream of riding the pony was right before her, yet out of reach. As the pony loaded onto its carriage and drove away, she couldn't help but feel a bit jealous of the other girls who got to experience it all. Tears welled up in her eyes as she hung her head in defeat. She couldn't understand why her dream was so close yet unattainable.

I'm Just Waiting On God's heart was heavy with regret, and she turned away from seeing others living out her dream. She felt sadness inside as she realized everyone else got to experience what she wanted most. Tears rolled down her face as she walked away, feeling left out and alone, waiting for something that never came.

HELP ME

The youngest sibling was excited as she rode the pink pony, her lengthy hair flying behind her in the wind. Help Me had invited several of her friends to join in on the fun, and they all took turns riding the pony with her. The sun beat down warmly on their faces as they laughed and cheered each other on.

As Help Me's turn returned, her friends gathered around to help her climb onto the pony. She grinned from ear to ear at the thought of riding once more surrounded by her closest friends. "There's nothing like friends," she exclaimed as she trotted around the yard.

This sibling saw no shame in accepting assistance from others. Help Me marveled at the view from atop the pony and felt like she was living a dream. "I did it!" she shouted, reveling in the moment.

But then Help Me fell off the pony, landing on the ground with a thud. Help Me's face twisted in confusion as She tried to get back on herself but realized she hadn't mastered mounting or dismounting on her own yet. "I thought this would be easy," she muttered, frustrated. "But I won't give up. I'll just call my friends back to help me."

TODAY COULD BE THE DAY

The sun shone brightly through the window, waking up Today Could Be The Day with excitement. Bursting into her siblings' rooms, she exclaimed, "Today could be the day we get our pony!" Her voice echoed off the walls as she jumped up and down in anticipation. "I'll make bows and brush its hair to make it even cuter!"

Later that afternoon, when their parents had the pink pony delivered to their home, Today Could Be The Day couldn't contain her joy. She ran to give thanks, hugging her parents tightly for such a wonderful gift. It was every little girl's dream to ride a pink pony, and now it was a reality.

she patiently waited while Help Me took her turn riding the pony. She watched with excitement as they giggled and played, unable to contain her eagerness for her turn. Finally, she stepped forward to take her turn but struggled to climb onto the pony's back. Determined, she tried repeatedly until finally, on her last attempt, she successfully mounted the pony.

Today Could Be The Day beamed with pride and joy at mastering the climb. She turned to one of her siblings, I'm Just Waiting on God, and said confidently, "Let me show you how to climb next."

But I'm Just Waiting on God; shook her head and replied, "No thanks; I'm just going to wait on God." Help Me, another sibling watching from afar with longing in her eyes spoke up. "I want to ride again," she pleaded.

Sadly, it was time for the day to end with the pony. But Today Could Be The Day was content and happy with how the day had turned out.

THE HAIRCUT

Time had passed, and the girls were now teenagers. One afternoon, the siblings sat together on the green grass in the backyard, discussing what they wanted to accomplish.

They stared at the three ladders in the backyard.

"Hey, have you ever wondered why our parents built those ladders?" I'm Just Waiting on God said.

"Nope, they've never said anything about them. I think it is weird," said Help Me.

"Maybe one day we will understand them," said Today Could Be The Day.

Help Me blurted out, "Let's change our appearances with new haircuts." The other siblings agreed. So, off they went to get their parent's approval for a trip to the salon. They walked into the living room, where they found their parents talking on the couch. Today Could Be The Day said, "We want new haircuts." The parents looked at each other and said simultaneously, "Yes!" That day, the siblings were on the way to the salon.

I'M JUST WAITING ON GOD

The sibling sat in the waiting area, unsure what haircut to get. After all, the sibling didn't want to get it wrong. She was looking at her phone, scrolling through haircuts that others wore. I'm Just Waiting on God was happy with all the possibilities of a new haircut.

But, just like all the other times, the sibling was hesitant and overcome with doubt. Perhaps I should just wait on God.

The excitement grew until Help Me came over with a new cut and asked I'm Just Waiting On God, "Why are you just sitting there and not getting a new cut? You always hesitate when it is time to do something and then blame it because you are just waiting on God. When will you decide on something? Anything?"

I'm Just Waiting on God sat there and looked at Help Me, wishing God would tell the sibling what to do next.

"I do want a new look," the sibling said. "But I'm just going to wait on God to show me what cut to get."

Saddened by her indecision and the pressure from her sibling, she left without a new haircut that day. She was even sadder after seeing how great the other siblings looked with their haircuts. She questioned why God had chosen to bless the others and not her that day.

HELP ME

Help me. I invited all her friends to help select a new haircut and style. They gathered around the siblings to take pictures, and everyone had input on the cut and style for Help Me.

"Don't worry. Help Me," one friend said. "We will ensure you get the best look of all."

"Oh, what would I do without my best friends to help me along the way? I have always depended on you to help with whatever I need.

It is great not to have to think or do the actual work. Life is great!" The sibling boasted.

Help Me left the salon with a great new haircut and style. Her friends came through once more to ensure her success.

TODAY COULD BE THE DAY

Today Could Be The Day thought about getting her haircut during the trip to the salon, brimming with excitement at the thought of something new.

This sibling had wanted a new cut for some time and was so happy that today could be the day for that dream to come true.

She scrolled through different pictures of haircuts and found none. She was determined not to give up despite not finding the right hairstyle.

She patiently waited for her turn and admired Help Me's friends' support in helping her choose a style.

Then, Today Could Be The Day's face lit up upon discovering the perfect cut. She presented the image to the stylist, saying, "This is exactly what I want."

In making this independent choice for herself that day at the salon, Today Could Be The Day learned an invaluable self-assurance lesson that would stay with her for years.

THE CLIMB

The sun was just beginning to set, casting a warm orange glow over the siblings as they gathered in their usual spot on a Saturday. The siblings had been meeting at the ladders for so long they had lost count of the previous years. It had become a gathering place of happy times for them weekly.

Today felt different. There was anticipation in the air, a feeling that something important would happen. The usually lively conversations were replaced with tense silence as if the ladders held their breath in anticipation.

"Have you ever wondered what it would be like to have a true purpose and meaning in your life?" one sibling asked, breaking the comfortable silence.

Another responded, "Well...I thought meeting here on Saturdays was enough, but now I desire more from my life."

A third said, "I believe it is time for us to do something different."

Their words hung in the air as they all looked at each other with determination. They were ready for their purpose to be revealed to each of them.

The siblings retired to their homes as usual as the night grew darker, but this evening would not be typical. Each one dreamt of standing in front of a tall ladder built by their parents.

In their dreams, they received their purpose while facing their ladder. But there were no clear instructions on how to reach the top. They were told to trust God and not doubt the process. However, they were also warned that they would be tempted to climb according to their desires.

When they woke up the next day and shared their dreams, two were eager to begin the journey, while another wanted to wait for further guidance from God.

But eventually, they all agreed to start together. Little did they know that their names reflected how they would approach their climb - chosen when they were younger based on their perspectives on life.

Today Could Be The Day took charge and declared, "We are starting this journey right now. We will meet at our ladders in an hour."

And so they began their journey together, unsure of what challenges lay ahead but determined to trust in God and each other.

I'M JUST WAITING ON GOD

I'm Just Waiting on God prayed for creative ideas about what to pursue. She received the ideas but never did anything with them.

This sibling seemed to complain about everything that was not understood. Often, when people try to get this sibling to do something differently, the sibling gets upset and says, "I am afraid that I will do the wrong thing. Therefore, I will just wait on God. So, leave me alone while I wait for God to tell me what to do next."

This sibling hated change and liked to control the environment and people around her. She refused to be uncomfortable, even knowing it was for the greater good. To her, being uncomfortable took her outside of her everyday life. So, no matter how many signs and signals would come from God, this sibling was set on remaining the same and allowing fear to rule.

She stood before the ladder, nervous but wanting to go for it anyway. One hand on the ladder and doubt suddenly entered the sibling's mind. I'm Just Waiting on God began to remember all the opportunities she missed growing up because she was waiting on God, which saddens her.

"Maybe those opportunities were not meant for me," I'm Just Waiting on God said, trying to convince herself that she missed nothing. But this time. The sibling wanted to climb the ladder more than ever. I'm Just Waiting on God was excited about the God-given ladder dream but still apprehensive about the climb.

The sibling took a deep breath and slowly began the climb. "This is not so bad," the sibling thought, "I thought it would be harder than this." I'm Just Waiting on God laughed. "I can do this!" the sibling said. Just then, I'm Just Waiting on God fell off the ladder.

"No!" the sibling cried out. "What happened? What did I do wrong?"

The sibling stared at the ladder for a moment and then sat at the bottom of her God-given ladder dream. She cried and said, "Maybe I should have just waited on God before I climbed. Now, I will do nothing at all but wait. In the meantime, I will tell others about my dream of a ladder."

The people heard the sibling's ladder dream and praised her for receiving such a dream. Many people wished they, too, could have a dream.

I'm Just Waiting on God prayed with others that God would give them a ladder dream. When some got their ladder dreams and conquered the climb, they called I'm Just Waiting on God to say thank you and that they had climbed their ladder dreams.

After hearing the news, I'm Just Waiting on God cried out with envy and jealousy of others who climbed their dreams. She asked God why He would give others ladder dreams and not allow her to accomplish her own. She faithfully showed up at the ladder dream every day with books, cell phone, and anything that would distract the sibling from climbing the ladder. I'm Just Waiting on God.

The other siblings asked why she was still sitting at the bottom of her ladder dream I'm Just Waiting On God said. "I can't climb because I have to read this book."

The next day, they asked the sibling again, and the response was, "I can't because I have to take a nap. I had a long day."

Every day, there was a different excuse, so the other siblings stopped asking and just looked away.

I'm Just Waiting on God called out to them occasionally. "Come sit with me."

The usual response received from the other siblings was "No." Shortly afterward, I'm Just Waiting on God silently rejoiced after seeing Today Could Be The Day get knocked off her ladder dream.

"See, if you just wait on God like me, you might make it.

This sibling daydreamed several times throughout the day about what it must feel like to achieve and enjoy the God-given ladder dream.

I'm Just Waiting on God cried out once more. "How long will I have to wait until I can climb again? Send me a sign to tell me when to climb my God-given ladder dream."

The other siblings realized that I'm Just Waiting On God's life was full of things to distract her from hearing God's voice.

Today Could Be The Day said, "Why don't you give up one thing and use that time to focus on climbing your God-given ladder dream?"

"No! I am just waiting on God to give me a sign," the sibling said. "Besides, these things define me, and I need them to feel important. I need people to call me for advice, and I must be available. Therefore, I will just wait on God to climb my ladder dream." The truth was that she was afraid to climb after failing the first time. And now comfort and distractions had become her best friends.

HELP ME

Help Me had many friends, but they were all chosen for their ability to help. No matter what task or desire arose, the sibling could call upon a friend, and they would come running to lend a hand. Due to this, Help Me never learned the important lesson of doing things independently. Whenever an idea struck, she would quickly enlist a friend to carry it out and then take credit for its success. For Help Me, life was all about partying and having fun.

"Okay, let's see how far I can get before I have to use another friend to carry me up the ladder," Help Me said. Her friends eagerly joined forces to create a makeshift window scraper adorned with colorful decorations like a party room. Together, they hoisted Help Me toward the top of her ladder dream as she sat like a queen, enjoying the ride and daily basking in her success. "Thank you for helping me," she would say with a carefree wave of her hand, proudly boasting to her friends about her achievements.

People marveled at her speed, but little did they know that it was all thanks to the hard work of her friends rather than her efforts. Looking down upon her fellow siblings - I'm Just Waiting on God and Today Could Be The Day - Help Me scoffed at their lack of progress. "You're so lazy and undeserving of your ladder dreams," she mocked. "God told us to climb no matter what, and you're just making excuses." She continued to flaunt her lavish lifestyle and a seemingly endless supply of money earned from her successful climb. "I'm throwing a big party tonight to celebrate my success," she announced. "I'm sure I'm Just Waiting on God will be there, as usual. But you, Today Could Be The Day, I won't even bother asking because I know you'll never come- you are too busy trying to climb your ladder dream."

But as Help Me reached the top of her ladder dreams faster than her siblings, she soon realized she didn't have the wisdom, knowledge, or understanding of what it took to stay at the top of her ladder dream. After all, she had never climbed on her own. "What am I supposed to do now?" she asked in frustration. "I thought this would be easy. I didn't realize there would still be work once I arrived." And with that, she continued her ways - partying and squandering her blessings on pleasures and gifts for those who helped her along the way.

One fateful night, while dancing at another extravagant party, Help Me lost her footing and fell from the top of her God-given ladder dream. As she tumbled to the bottom, she realized she hadn't learned any valuable lessons during her climb. Looking up at the ladder above her again, she knew that without true character, she would never be able to remain at the top of her God-given ladder dream. Help Me could not show anyone else how to climb because she had never learned to climb, Nor could she climb her God-given ladder dream on her own.

TODAY COULD BE THE DAY

The presence of this particular sibling always brought a buzz of excitement to the room. She radiated joy and ambition, constantly setting goals and achieving them. Though she enjoyed spending time with her friends, she found the most peace in moments spent with God. Her presence was a pleasure to be around.

As she woke up each morning, filled with eager anticipation for what the day could bring, her infectious enthusiasm spread to those around her. "Today could be the day," she often declared, referring to her God-given ladder dream that she was determined to climb.

With a smile and words of encouragement, she stood at the base of the ladder and urged her siblings to join her in their climb. "We can do it!" she exclaimed, overflowing with excitement.

But as they began to climb together, Today Could Be The Day slipped and fell off the ladder. It wasn't what she had imagined - she had hoped to climb alongside her siblings towards their shared dream.

But as she looked at her siblings, she saw I'm Just Waiting on God sitting at the bottom of the ladder. Seeing Help Me pass by with their friends, Today Could Be The Day realized that sometimes you must continue your journey alone. "I thought we would climb our God-given ladder dream together," she thought sadly.

When she initially shared her dream with her friends, they dismissed it as too hard or questioned whether God truly wanted her to pursue it. They didn't want to be a part of the process. Yet now, from a comfortable distance, they watched in awe and waited to see if Today Could Be The Day would make it. "We'll come back into your life if you make it," they said.

Despite feeling disappointed and abandoned, Today Could Be The Day pressed on toward her dream. She knew that, in the end, only she and God truly mattered on this climb.

Though her heart was heavy, Today Could Be The Day knew she had to continue the climb alone. She returned up the ladder with renewed determination and faith in God's plan. Today could be the day she reaches the top, and nothing - not even the absence of her friends - could stop her from pursuing her God-given dream with all her heart.

The sibling still got up, excited to climb each day. There was one thing that kept the sibling going. There was a meeting with God for prayer at the beginning of each day before the climb. "God, I ask for the wisdom and endurance to climb each day and to learn whatever I need to keep me there when I reach my God-given ladder dream. Also, show me how to help others to climb as well. AMEN"

Today Could Be The Day fell off the ladder the next day after being informed of bad news that freed up more time in her life. Instead of being upset for long periods of time, the sibling used the time to climb longer, and Today Could Be the Day continued climbing.

A week later, it was discovered that the car was missing. "How will I get to the ladder now?" Today Could Be the Day, said. "I know. I will use this time to exercise. I will walk to the ladder each day."

Time passed, and the sibling could not climb yet again. She dislocated her left knee while walking to the ladder. "I cannot stop now! It hurts, but I am still excited and must keep going."

One person showed up, and Today Could Be The Day asked, "Can I lean on you for a moment to help me get to the ladder?"

The kind stranger helped but said, "I'm not here to stay; I only came to help you get to the ladder." Today Could Be The Day stayed on the ladder looking over at I Am Just Waiting On God – who was smirking.

"Oh, let's see you continue the climb now," said I'm Just Waiting On God. Finally, "I will not be alone here, not climbing my God-given ladder dream."

Today Could Be the Day, I thought. "Today could be the day that I reach my God-given ladder dream. I can't give up now. I feel like I am so close to finishing." The sibling continued the climb with pain.

When I'm Just Waiting on God saw Today Could Be The Day climb even though she was injured, the sibling cried out to God again. "Why can't I climb my God-given ladder dream?"

The sibling looked over and said, I'm Just Waiting on God, "Come on." But the sibling said, no, I am just waiting on God.

Today Could Be The Day knew that God had given her a ladder dream that needed accomplishing. It would be challenging, but God had shown the ending, which was great!

The sibling took notes of her failures and successes. "I will use what I need and toss out the rest," Today Could Be The Day said. "I will not hold on to bitterness or anger because of my failures."

After numerous failures, the sibling reached the God-given ladder dream. She had physical and spiritual strength and looked physically different. The mental strength came from the constant prayers and casting down of negative thoughts that tried to keep her from climbing.

Today Could Be The Day could now encourage and pray with others to do what she did. The sibling knew the voice of the Lord because she had heard it many times along the climb. The physical strength came. She had developed physical shape along the way.

Today Could Be The Day wanted a purpose and to live her God-given ladder dream. Part of the process of climbing the ladder dream included failing several times while attempting to climb because it took faith to continue to get back up. Once the resilience was built up, getting knocked off didn't hurt as much. Today Could Be The Day uses strength, endurance, and self-confidence to travel up and down the ladder and help others climb their God-given ladder dreams.

THE TRUTH

THE LADDER

The ladder represents truth; it is the sense of urgency that you feel in your body that something more is required of you. You say, "I'm so frustrated with my life." And "I know there has to be more to life than this."

If this is you, then you are standing at the bottom of your ladder dream. The ladder is when you are still determining what you want to do or how to get there. It disrupts your sleep at night. This ladder marks a place where uncertainty lingers.

You will often wake up at the same time each night. This is where you just wake up and listen. Get up pray, listen to God, get coffee or tea, play music, clean, just get up. Even if you return to your sleep. It's a silent call to action, urging you to rise and engage with the world around you. Whether brewing a cup of coffee or losing yourself in music, these moments demand acknowledgment. By embracing this restlessness, you open the door to something greater, something profound waiting on the horizon— The dream will come next.

THE DREAM

It can come at any time of the day or night. The dream is your purpose calling you. Giving you bits and pieces of information to keep you moving forward. People may not believe in your dream at this stage; it is okay; it is not their responsibility to believe in something given to you.

When you take responsibility for the dream, protect it, write it down, and work on it, more responsibility will come to you. This dream is not just a thought but a persistent calling that speaks directly to you. It is the essence of your purpose, the seed from which all else will grow.

Do not let doubts or criticisms from others dim its light. This dream is yours to pursue.

But do not mistake this dream for an easy path. It will demand effort and sacrifices from you. You must be willing to labor towards its fulfillment and face obstacles head-on.

However, more opportunities will come with each step closer to this dream.

This dream is not just a destination but a journey that will shape and transform you into the person you are meant to become.

So, hold onto this dream tightly and let it guide you towards your purpose in life, your life's work.

The dream is the activation.

THE CLIMB

The climb is all about the approach. How you approach your dream matters. Decide that you will work on your dreams no matter the situation and circumstances that may come against you. When you learn to do the work; you will always know how to climb.

The climb to achieving your dreams is not easy. It requires hard work, dedication, and perseverance. There will be many obstacles and challenges, but how you approach them will determine your success.

Your mindset toward your dream is crucial. If you see it as an impossible task or allow self-doubt to creep in, you set yourself up for failure. But if you believe in yourself and have a positive attitude, nothing can stop you from reaching the top. No matter how often you fail, roll over and get back up—KEEP GOING!

However, commitment also means being flexible. Sometimes, our dreams may shift or evolve along the way, and adjusting our approach is important.

You cannot expect success without the work. This may require learning new skills or improving existing ones, but anything is possible with determination and practice.

While there will be setbacks and failures along the way, remember that these are opportunities for growth and learning. Embrace them as a chance to improve yourself and your approach to achieving your dreams.

Lastly, always remember that there is no one clear path to success. Each person's journey will look different, but as long as you stay true to yourself and remain focused on your dreams, you will always find a way.

So, keep climbing. And when you reach your destination, take a moment to reflect on all that you have overcome and accomplished.

Because in the end, it's not just about you.

I'M JUST WAITING ON GOD

I'm Just Waiting on God believes that God will speak to her and give her instructions on every detail in her life without communication with Him. She uses *"I'm just waiting on God"* as an excuse to do nothing. She still expects things to happen in her life. I am just waiting on God means that you are just waiting on God and willing to do nothing yourself. He may not give you all the small details because there may be something that you need to acquire or let go of before you get to what he has shown you. So, get up and make a choice, even if it is the wrong one. God will guide you into what He showed. That bad decision may be part of your growth and the journey.

This sibling uses that as an excuse not to decide for fear that she will make the wrong one. Once God gave the sibling the dream to climb the ladder, it was the sibling's responsibility to do all that could be done to get to the top.

If you are an *"I'm just waiting on God"* person, then invite God into every area of your life and then trust that He is there every time you decide in life. God is not your puppet master while you sit and be the puppet. You can wait on God for a lifetime and watch your dreams lived by someone who decided to do something.

HELP ME

This sibling does not understand the value of doing it yourself and getting the growth out of that. There is nothing wrong with using the resources around you for assistance, but when you use them to do it entirely for you, you are not willing to do the work.

If you are a "Help Me," you should repent for using people and allow them to be with you and not in the gap for you. You may want to set small goals and accomplish them to uplift your confidence.

TODAY COULD BE THE DAY

This sibling is optimistic about everything in life because they understand it is a choice. Many people do not understand this person. They feel they are faking it because nobody can be that happy all the time. Initially, it is a daily fight to stay with faith over fear. However, it becomes easier every day, and it becomes a lifestyle.

When faith is a way of life, you can encourage others. Your determination will always make you stronger. Also, each time you climb, you are getting a step closer, which keeps you going. Finally, you reach your goals and now live the vision that God showed you. You understand the climb and encourage others to climb because you understand the gift of doing the work to follow your God-given ladder dream.

The Ladder, The Dream, and the Climb.

About Author

Tambeara Watkins was born and raised in Atlanta, Georgia. She enjoys her family, outdoor activities, designing, coffee, and writing.

www.ingramcontent.com/pod-product-compliance
Lightning Source LLC
Chambersburg PA
CBHW070253310726
48976CB00008B/2642